GODZILLA™

Adapted by James Preller

Based on the screenplay
by Dean Devlin
& Roland Emmerich

ISBN 0-590-57213-X

Designed by Madalina Stefan

12 11 10 9 8 7 6 5 4 3 2 1   8 9/9 0 1 2 3/0

Printed in the U.S.A.
First Scholastic printing, June 1998

It Begins...

All was calm on the beautiful Moruroa Atoll Islands. Waves from the Pacific Ocean lapped against sandy beaches. In the interior forest, animals thrived. Here was the home of some of the world's most exotic creatures: Komodo dragons, Gila monsters, lizards, chameleons, and more.

But the early morning peace was soon broken. A voice counted down, "Five...four... three...two...one."

A blinding flash of light shattered the scene. A nuclear explosion mushroomed into the sky. Then another explosion. Then another. For here was the place where the French government had chosen to test the world's deadliest weapon: the atomic bomb.

Radioactive waste fell from the sky. It fell on the ocean, on plants, and on beaches. It fell on all things — on nests and eggs, burying creatures both alive and yet to be born. Then all was still once more.

A new terror had been born.

Attack at Sea...

Time passed; years rolled on. The nuclear tests were now a sad history, long forgotten.

Aboard a Japanese fishing tanker, a sailor steadied the immense craft in a rough sea. The boat, brimming with fish, headed back to port.

Suddenly, a warning signal blared. The sailor checked the sonar. He saw a large, dark mass heading toward the ship.

"Captain," he called. "We have an emergency."

Instantly, the ship was rocked. It swayed violently, throwing crew members to the floor.

"What was that?!" the captain asked.

"We must have hit something...." the sailor replied.

The two men could barely see out the rain-streaked window. Something was out there, something dangerous. But what could it be?

The ship was hit again and again. Then an enormous set of claws ripped into the steel hull. Water flooded in, causing the ship to founder on its side.

In the dark of the night, a huge figure rose from the water. He let out the eerie cry of a tormented creature — a blood-chilling wail.

"Singing in the Mud"

Meanwhile, at the site of the infamous nuclear accident in Chernobyl, Ukraine, a research scientist by the name of Dr. Niko Tatopoulos cheerfully drove his utility van. Nick, as he preferred to be called, wore a Walkman and sang aloud with it.

Nick paused briefly near a sign that read in Russian: *NO TRESPASSING. NUCLEAR RADIATION.* Nick drove on. He had permission to be there.

The van slid to a stop in a muddy field, beside the dangerous nuclear power plant. Nick quickly set to work. He grabbed metal cases from the back of the van. He drove spikes into the ground. Adjusting the dials of a box, Nick sent electric shock waves into the earth.

In an instant, dozens of worms crawled to the surface. As he worked, Nick continued singing. "I'm singing in the mud, just scooping up my worms...."

When a military helicopter landed nearby, Nick turned to see a man in a long raincoat hurrying toward him.

"Dr. Niko Topopolosis?"

"It's Tatopoulos," Nick corrected. "What's going on?"

"The worm guy, right?" The man reached out to shake Nick's hand. "You've been reassigned."

"Gojira...Gojira...Gojira!"

Phillipe Roache stood outside a hospital in Tahiti. Dark and intense, he paused to gather his thoughts.

"Are there any survivors?" he asked.

"Only one, sir," his assistant, Jean-Claude, replied.

Inside the hospital, Phillipe peered through an open door. He saw the survivor, the old cook from the fishing tanker, curled up on a bed. With a commanding gesture, Phillipe cleared the room. His men set up video-recording equipment.

The old cook stared into space, frozen with fear.

Jean-Claude remarked, "Whatever happened to him on that ship put him in a complete state of shock."

Phillipe brought the flame from his cigarette lighter close to the cook's face. He whispered, "What did you see, old man?"

A flicker of recognition crossed the cook's face, as if remembering a nightmare. At last he spoke. One single word, a name, repeated over and over.

"Gojira...Gojira...Gojira! GOJIRA!!"

"Standing Inside a Footprint"

Nick stepped out of a seaplane to find himself in a small fishing village in Panama. The place was in ruins, swarming with military, media, and police.

Colonel Alex Hicks greeted Nick on the pier. Hicks led Nick into the jungle.

"Do you know that you just interrupted a three-year study of the Chernobyl earthworm?" Nick complained. "The radioactive contamination in that area mutated the earthworm's DNA! You have any idea what that means?"

Hicks sighed. "No, but I have the feeling I'm about to find out."

"It means that due to a man-made radiation accident, the Chernobyl earthworms are now over seventeen percent larger than they were before!"

Hicks wasn't impressed. "Seventeen percent? Sounds big."

"That's enormous!" Nick exclaimed. "That's what I've been trying to tell you. I'm only a biologist. I take radioactive samples and study them."

Hicks pointed to the ground. "Great. Here's your sample. Study it."

Nick was confused. "What sample?" he asked. "Where is it?" Finally, Nick recognized that he was standing in a gigantic footprint. It was 45 feet long.

Back in the village, Nick caught up with Colonel Hicks. "That was a footprint," Nick exclaimed. "I was standing *inside* a footprint!"

Hicks answered, "That's right."

Nick shook his head. "But there's no animal in the world that can make footprints like that." A wave of doubt crossed his face. "Is there?"

Dr. Elsie Chapman joined the conversation. Elsie was head of the research team. Hicks explained that no one saw what made the footprints. No one knew what destroyed the village. Only one thing was certain.

It was very big...very fast...and very dangerous.

Audrey Timmonds, Cub Reporter

On Manhattan Island, New York City, Audrey Timmonds began another workday at the WIDF television station. More than anything, Audrey wanted to become a reporter. She was good, and she knew it. But so far, she had not been given the chance to prove herself.

To make things worse, her boss, anchorman Charles Caiman, was a total sleaze. But Audrey still hoped for a promotion. She rushed up to Caiman. She wanted to learn if she'd gotten the new job as a reporter.

"Did you talk with Humphries?" Audrey asked. Humphries was the man who made the final decisions. Audrey knew that Caiman had a lot of influence with him.

Caiman answered, "It's between you and Rodriguez."

Audrey was thrilled. "What else did he say?"

Instead of answering, Caiman asked Audrey out on a date — even though he was married.

Audrey ignored the invitation. She pleaded, "Mr. Caiman, I've been doing extra research for you for over three years. I'm too old to be your assistant anymore."

"So have dinner with me tonight," Caiman said.

"I can't."

Caiman shrugged. "It's your choice," he said...and walked away.

Nick Finds a Clue

After the trip to Panama, Nick was flown to the Caribbean island of Jamaica. On shore, Nick and Elsie joined Colonel Hicks to examine the latest casualty — the Japanese tanker with two holes ripped into its hull.

Strangely, three unknown men were already there, taking measurements of the ship. Nick didn't know it, but they were the same men from the hospital in Tahiti.

Hicks angrily pointed. "Lieutenant, get those people away from there."

A man stepped forward. "They are with me." It was Phillipe Roache. He handed Hicks a card and explained that he was from an insurance agency, there to inspect the damaged ship.

Hicks was suspicious.

Phillipe persisted. "Colonel, what do you think could have done this?"

Hicks was in no mood to answer questions. He barked, "Get your people out of there or I will."

Meanwhile, Nick surveyed the wreckage. Cans of tuna lay scattered on the beach. He spotted something unusual near the gash in the ship. Nick pulled out a pair of tweezers. He removed what appeared to be a chunk of reptile flesh.

No one noticed.

No one, that is, except for Phillipe Roache.

"Dawn of a New Species"

Aboard a military transport plane, Colonel Hicks received more bad news. A soldier informed him, "Colonel, we just got a report of three fishing trawlers being pulled down."

Hicks checked a map, tracing his finger where all the incidents had occurred. He said, "It's only two hundred miles off the American eastern seaboard and we don't even know what it is."

Elsie offered a theory. "*Theropoda allosaurus*," she said. "A type of enormous reptile the likes of which we believe died out in the Cretaceous period."

Nick was doubtful. He looked up from his microscope, where he had been examining the reptilian flesh. "What about the traces of radiation?"

All eyes turned to Nick. He explained, "This creature is far too large to be some lost dinosaur."

Nick continued, "It was first sighted off the French Polynesian Pacific coast — an area that has been exposed to dozens of nuclear tests over the last thirty years."

Nick believed the creature was a mutant created by the radioactive fallout from the long-ago tests.

"Like your earthworms?" Elsie asked.

"Yes!" Nick answered. "We're looking at the dawn of a new species. The first of its kind."

Meanwhile, something dark and mysterious moved swiftly through the water. It was headed for Manhattan.

"First Rule of the Jungle"

Audrey Timmonds joined her friends and coworkers, a cameraman nicknamed Animal and his wife, Lucy, at a Manhattan diner. She was still upset with Caiman.

Lucy told her, "Audrey, you're too nice, that's your problem. You gotta be a killer to get ahead. I'm sorry, baby, but you just don't have what it takes."

Doubtful, Audrey asked Animal, "You don't think that's true?"

Animal nodded. "Nice guys finish last. First rule of the jungle."

Maybe they were right, Audrey considered. Maybe it *was* time to get tough. Just then she noticed a familiar face on the television above the counter.

"It's Nick!" she exclaimed.

The news story showed Nick walking with Colonel Hicks in Panama.

"Who is he?" Lucy asked.

"My college sweetie!" Audrey exclaimed. "He looks so handsome on TV."

Lucy was curious. "Did Romeo have a name?"

"Niko Tatopoulos."

Animal smirked. "That why you dumped him?"

"No!" Audrey answered. "I just couldn't see myself with some boring egghead who spends his summer picking apart cockroaches."

Audrey explained that she and Nick had once been a steady couple for nearly four years.

Lucy exclaimed, "Girl, I'm surprised he didn't ask you to marry him."

"That's the problem," Audrey answered. "He did."

The Creature Attacks

A typical, hustle-bustle day in Manhattan. Joggers went for their morning runs, motorists honked and complained as they flocked downtown, and a lonely fisherman cast his line off the end of a pier.

Suddenly, the dock seemed to lift straight up! Bursting out of the water, the creature's talons gripped the land's edge. A wave of water crashed down as the enormous reptile climbed out of the water.

Drivers swerved and crashed. People screamed and ran. The creature sniffed the air. His enormous jaw chomped down on a truck loaded with fish, lifting it high into the air.

Nearby, Mayor Ebert was giving a speech. Ever so faintly, the crowd of spectators began to notice a soft thumping sound. It grew louder. Heads turned. What could it be?

The mayor droned on. "The city is a safer place today...."

One by one, buildings began to fall like dominoes. Fear gripped the crowd.

"What is that noise?" the mayor asked an aide.

A massive leg came down on cars, flattening them. The reptile moved quickly, effortlessly. Then a giant tail smashed the columns of city hall. The stone building crumbled as if it were paper.

Animal Takes a Picture

The creature — terrifying and unstoppable — marched through the city streets, destroying all in his path.

Inside the diner where Audrey and her friends sat, a distant thunder could be heard.

Lucy noticed the noise and muttered, "Tell me that's not another parade."

"I don't think that's a parade," Animal answered.

Plates and glasses began to shake and fall to the floor. Outside the window, a mob of people raced past, screaming as they ran.

Without hesitation, Animal charged out the door to get his camera. He saw a city in ruins: hydrants sprayed water, cars burned, bricks fell from the sky.

Animal grabbed his video camera from the WIDF news van. He was a cameraman, totally fearless, and this was going to be the picture of a lifetime.

Stepping into the street, Animal saw the massive reptile come directly toward him. Animal raised his camera — only to see a giant foot come crashing down on him.

It was all over — he thought.

But no deathblow came. Amazingly, Animal still stood, breathless and frozen, in the space *between the creature's toes*!

"He Just...Disappeared"

The bad news just got worse. In his command tent across the river in New Jersey, Colonel Hicks learned that the city was being evacuated. It wasn't safe for anyone. But remarkably — the creature had vanished.

Sergeant O'Neal stammered to explain. "He just... *disappeared*."

Elsie suggested that the creature probably returned to the water.

Nick wasn't so sure. Looking across the river to the vast Manhattan skyline, he said, "I don't think so. He came to New York for a reason. This is a place where he can easily hide."

Nick paused. "He's in there someplace."

Audrey Takes a Risk

Audrey saw her chance to earn her stripes as a full-fledged reporter. She raced up to Caiman at the studio.

"Mr. Caiman, I've got a lead," she announced. "I know a guy on the inside with the military."

Caiman wasn't listening. This was *his* story — and he wasn't about to share the glory with Audrey.

Frustrated and angry, Audrey remembered Lucy's words: *"Audrey, you're too nice, that's your problem."*

Well, Audrey figured, nice guys finish last. So she stole Caiman's press pass. After all, as Lucy had pointed out, how often are you going to have an ex-boyfriend on the inside of a major story?

Meanwhile, a group of foreign men with high-tech equipment watched all. They viewed television monitors. They listened in on private conversations between the mayor and the military.

Phillipe Roache sipped a cup of coffee. He watched…and he waited.

The Trap Is Set

While searching the city, soldiers discovered that Nick's theory was right. The creature hadn't returned to the sea. Instead, he had tunneled into the 23rd Street subway station. He was in there somewhere, silently lurking.

Nick had an idea. He told Colonel Hicks, "When I needed to catch earthworms, I knew the best way was not to *dig* them out, but *draw* them out."

How? To catch a mouse, you set a trap with cheese. To catch this creature, fish would be the bait. After all, it seemed to be going after fish during every previous attack.

So the trap was set. The military dumped a load of fish outside the subway tunnel. But would the creature take the bait?

Tense with fear, soldiers lined up, armed and ready. Suddenly, a deafening roar pierced the stillness. The street cracked. The creature, massive and thickly muscled, rose from the ground. The soldiers aimed their weapons and waited for a signal.

"Fire at will!" Hicks ordered.

Bullets and missiles hit the great beast. Yet he seemed unhurt, more annoyed than injured.

Amazingly fast, the creature leaped behind a building. Armored vehicles skidded around corners in hot pursuit, firing as they went. The creature swiftly turned. With a gust of wind, his powerful lungs blew the vehicles helplessly backward.

A fleet of Apache helicopters swooped down and gave chase. The pilot checked in. "We have him, locked on."

The rockets fired. Buildings on all sides burst into flame like matchsticks. But again the creature evaded the weapons. The pilot informed Hicks, "The heat seekers can't lock. He's colder than the buildings around him."

Once again, the creature mysteriously vanished. He camouflaged himself, blending into the background as he stood upright in a gutted skyscraper.

Like a cat playing with toys, the creature reappeared and swiped at the helicopters, destroying one, then another, then another. One minute he was there — *swallowing a helicopter whole!* — and the next moment, gone.

Later, Nick walked amid the ruins. Fires burned. Buildings tumbled. Nick noticed a pool of reddish-brown goo. He scooped up a sample. At least now they'd learn a little more about this strange, new enemy.

"He's Pregnant!"

Nick had a theory. Outside Central Command, he stopped at a pharmacy and picked up some home pregnancy tests.

A voice behind him said, "It's good to see you, Nick."

"Audrey?!" Nick was staggered. He noticed her fake press pass and mistakenly assumed she had become a reporter. "So you've made it. I'm happy for you."

Audrey shrugged. "Yeah, well. You still picking apart cockroaches?"

All the old anger and hurt flooded back to Nick. He snapped, "I'm into earthworms now. But I don't want to *bore you* with my work."

"You're still mad at me," Audrey said.

"Well," Nick answered, "you left me without a phone call, a letter, nothing."

Saddened, Audrey turned to walk away.

"Audrey, wait," Nick called. "Eight years is a long time. Can I offer you a cup of tea?"

The two old friends walked back to Nick's tent inside the Central Command compound. Nick explained his theory about the creature. After testing the blood sample, Nick announced, "He's pregnant."

"I don't get it," Audrey said. "If he's the first of his kind, how can he be pregnant? Doesn't he need a mate?"

Nick explained that sometimes — in rare circumstances — animals can reproduce without a mate. It was definitely a scientific possibility.

He told Audrey, "I kept wondering why he would travel all this way. But it makes perfect sense. All kinds of creatures have been known to go great distances for reproduction. That's why he came to New York — he's nesting!"

Nick rushed away to the military lab for further tests, leaving Audrey alone in his tent. While waiting, Audrey noticed a video labeled *First Sighting.* Curious, she popped it into the VCR and saw shots of the Japanese cook in the hospital...footprints in Panama...and a destroyed tanker in Jamaica.

Here was Audrey's big chance. She knew it was wrong to steal the tape, but she also figured it was her ticket to stardom. It might make her career. Audrey recalled Animal's advice — *"Nice guys finish last"* — and rushed back to the station.
The tape was hidden in her purse.

Audrey's Betrayal

In a small motel room, Phillipe Roache and his men watched their monitors. They secretly observed a conference taking place at the command tent.

While top officials debated strategy, Nick interrupted to inform them that the creature was about to lay eggs, if he hadn't already. He urged, "We have to find the nest. If we don't, dozens more will be born, each one capable of laying eggs on its own."

Nick believed that it was urgent to find the nest and destroy the eggs. If they didn't act soon, dozens of creatures could overrun the city.

The debate stopped when the governor gestured to a television. Onscreen, Charles Caiman aired the video that Audrey had stolen from Nick's tent. Caiman betrayed Audrey, taking all the credit for himself. He announced, "From an old Japanese sailor's song about a mythological sea dragon who attacked sailors to our own modern-day terror. Who is this Godzilla, where did he come from, and why is he here? Find out in my special report."

The military men, General Anderson, Colonel Hicks, and Sergeant O'Neal were furious.
O'Neal looked at Nick accusingly.

Hicks angrily blamed Nick for giving a copy of the tape to the press.

Nick was confused. He shook his head. "No, it's still in my tent." Then, a sickening
thought entered his mind. "Oh my god, she *took* it."

It was General Anderson who fired Nick—on the spot. "Pack your stuff. You're officially off this project as of now."

Back in his motel room, Phillipe snapped off the television. He stared out the window, thinking.

"We're leaving," he announced.

Hijacked!

Humiliated, Nick quickly packed and left his tent. But not before ripping up some old photos of himself and Audrey.

Audrey saw Nick waiting for a cab. "You're leaving?" she asked.

Nick slammed his bags into the trunk of a cab.

"Is this because of me?" Audrey cried. "Because of the story?"

Nick stared in anger. "You're supposed to be my friend," he said. "I trusted you."

A few feet away, but unseen, Animal listened to their conversation.

Audrey tried to explain. "Look, I lied to you. I'm not a reporter. That's why I needed this story so bad. I just couldn't tell you I'm a failure."

Nick got into the cab. "So you thought that made it okay to steal my tape? Good luck in your new career. I think you really have what it takes."

The cab raced off into the night. Audrey stood alone in her misery. Rain, or tears, streaked her face.

Animal wanted to help. He jumped into his van and followed the cab.

After a few minutes, Nick noticed that the driver had missed a turn. "I don't think this is the way to the airport," he said.

The doors locked shut. The driver brought the cab to a sharp halt. He turned to Nick, who recognized the man's face. "Hey, I know you. You're that insurance guy."

The driver showed Nick a badge. "Agent Phillipe Roache. The French Secret Service," Phillipe said. "I thought you might like to know that your American friends have decided not to look for the creature's nest."

"How do you know?" Nick asked.

"We know," Phillipe replied. "Trust me."

Nick was uncertain. He had trusted Audrey and it had only made things worse. He didn't want to make the same mistake again. "Trust you!" he exclaimed. "Why would I do that?"

Phillipe answered, "Because you're the only one who wants to find the nest as much as I do."

A warehouse door opened and Phillipe pulled the car inside. Animal parked nearby and looked through a window. The warehouse was filled with Phillipe's support team. It was stocked with radios, guns, explosives, and armored vehicles.

Phillipe told Nick that he wanted to find Godzilla's nest. But he needed Nick's help.

The Frenchman confided, "I love my country. Can you understand that? It is my job to protect my country. Sometimes I must even protect it from itself, from mistakes we have made. Mistakes that we do not want the world to know about."

Nick replied, "You are talking about the nuclear testing in the Pacific."

"Yes," Phillipe answered. "This testing done by my country left a terrible mess. We are here to clean it up."

But time was running out. Phillipe needed an answer. "So you're in?" he asked.

Nick was determined to get back into the hunt. "Are you kidding? I always wanted to join the French Foreign Legion."

Nowhere to Hide

Animal raced back to find Audrey. He wanted her to go with him to follow Nick. She could help show the world that Nick was right. And maybe, just maybe, she could regain his trust.

In the meantime, Nick, Phillipe, and Phillipe's men went back to the subway station where they believed Godzilla's nest might be.

Following them, Animal and Audrey entered the subway tunnel. Ahead of them, Nick, Phillipe, and the French team followed a trail of fish deeper into the dank tunnel.

They stopped. The ground quaked. Suddenly, Godzilla burst through the wall, his huge claws burrowing forward. Godzilla paid no attention to them. He was after something else.

Above the tunnel, the military had set another trap. They piled fish into a large meadow in Central Park, knowing that the smell would lure the creature into open space.

This time Godzilla would have nowhere to hide.

Godzilla emerged from the tunnel and headed toward the trap. Nearing the park, the creature hesitated, uncertain. Some ancient instinct warned him: *Something was not right.*

Still, Godzilla moved cautiously forward.

Finally, the command came. "Fire at will!"

The military fired everything they had. Missiles launched. Apache helicopters poured down from the sky. Godzilla turned and ran. Desperate, he leaped and hurled himself into the river...and disappeared below the surface.

Three nuclear submarines lay in wait. They converged on the target. Godzilla swiped at one, destroying it. A cornered animal, Godzilla tried to escape by digging his way back into Manhattan.

A torpedo sped through the water. "Direct hit," a soldier called out triumphantly as the torpedo ripped into its target.

Slowly, silently, the creature known as Godzilla drifted motionlessly through the water. Down he fell, down into the river's black depths.

No known creature could have survived such a blast.

The Nest

Everything depended upon Nick and Phillipe. They were the only ones who believed Godzilla had a nest. They alone knew the eggs must be destroyed.

The trail from the subway led to Madison Square Garden, a huge arena that was used for rock concerts and sports events.

Flashlight beams cut through the dark, sending eerie slivers of light into the pitch-blackness. Nick saw something unusual.

"Three eggs," Nick said, surprised. "I thought there would be more."

Jean-Claude directed his beam into another area. "You were right." *Hundreds of eggs* filled the arena floor!

Phillipe's men snapped into action. Working quickly, the team laid out explosives around the eggs. But there was not enough time.

Phillipe and Nick heard something stir inside an egg. It cracked loudly as a new baby struggled for freedom. Then more eggs hatched, and more. The hungry Baby Godzillas gobbled up fish. Then they turned their attention to a more entertaining snack: *live food*.

Phillipe shouted orders into the radio. "Everyone outside! NOW!"

No Way Out

Unknown to Nick and Phillipe, Audrey and Animal had also found the nest. It soon grew too dangerous to be there. Audrey narrowly escaped the grip of one of the babies. She and Animal ran into a locker room and slammed the door.

The Baby Godzillas swarmed like sharks, starving for food. The door would not hold for long. Animal and Audrey climbed up through an air vent. They were safe, at least for now.

Meanwhile, Nick and Phillipe raced through the corridors, pausing only to seal the doorways.

Jean-Claude caught up with Phillipe. He reported, "We've secured the doors on the upper levels."

Phillipe was concerned about the other members of his crew. "Where are the rest of my men?"

"They didn't make it," Jean-Claude answered.

Phillipe took a deep breath. He turned to Nick. "Jean-Claude and I will hold them here. You will have to go and get help!"

Phillipe and Jean-Claude snapped together rifles and took their positions. But the Baby Godzillas broke through every door and smashed every barrier.

Nick's heart pounded as he searched for an exit. He heard a loud crash, then another. Baby Godzillas gathered at each end of the hallway.

Nick was trapped.

Or was he? He dove for an elevator call button. "Come on, come on," he urged, willing the doors to open.

At the last possible second, the elevator doors slid open. Nick made it! But he had learned a terrible thing: There seemed to be no way out.

"Destroy This Building!"

Crawling through the air vent, Animal glimpsed Phillipe below. Animal aimed his camera and began to film what he saw.

Nick returned. Breathless, he told Phillipe, "They're all over the place. I couldn't get out."

Crash! The vent collapsed. Animal and Audrey came tumbling down.

"It's okay," Nick told Phillipe. "I know her."

There was no time for introductions. A hungry pack of Baby Godzillas slammed against the nearest locked door.

Phillipe thought hard, trying to form a plan. They had no radio to the outside, no walkie-talkies. The phone lines were jammed. There was no way to send a message.

"I know a way," Audrey volunteered. With the ravenous Baby Godzillas hot on their heels, Audrey led the men into a broadcast booth, which was used to televise hockey games. She booted up the computer and explained, "It's a direct feed into our station's computer system."

"We'll broadcast from here," Animal said. He grabbed a camera and trained it on the babies clawing outside the door.

On television screens throughout the city, Audrey reported. "We're live from inside Madison Square Garden where Dr. Niko Tatopoulos has discovered the beast's lair. Doctor, tell us what is happening here."

"We've discovered over two hundred eggs, which began hatching only moments ago. If the military is listening, they must immediately destroy this building before the Baby Godzillas can escape!"

The pack clawed at the door, feverishly trying to reach its prey. Audrey screamed.

"Oh, my god! They're coming!"

"Party's Over"

"Okay, party's over!" Phillipe announced. He sprayed bullets through a window. Phillipe tossed a spool of cable far below. "Anyone care to join me?"

Climbing down, Audrey kissed Nick. "In case I can't later," she explained.

Phillipe led the way to the escalators. The exit was just down the stairs, but the path was blocked. Dozens of babies gathered in the lobby, scavenging the concession stands for food.

Phillipe saw three large chandeliers hanging in a line between himself and the front door. He fired a short burst, slicing the cable. The first chandelier shattered on the pack below. "Let's go," Phillipe said. As they ran, Phillipe made a path by shooting the second, then the third chandelier. Each time one fell, the animals were trapped underneath it.

High above, a squadron of F-18s raced to the city. The lead bomber broke formation, slicing low over the rooftops. The army had heard Audrey's report. They had come to destroy Madison Square Garden and its ferocious invaders, the Baby Godzillas.

Phillipe was the last one out. Audrey, Nick, and Animal were also safe. No one from Phillipe's team survived.

A huge explosion ripped into the building, sending a mountain of flames into the sky. First there was screaming — hundreds of newborn babies calling out in pain and fear — then silence. The silence of the dead.

Nick touched Audrey's cheek. They kissed. "Are you okay?"

A loud, mournful cry broke the peace. Godzilla had returned! The creature nuzzled the burned remains of his young. Godzilla lifted his head, filled with hatred and rage.

Now he wanted revenge.

"What do we do now?" Animal asked.

"Running," Phillipe suggested, "would be a good idea."

The Final Chase

Phillipe led the team through an alley. They climbed into an empty cab and raced off.

The cab narrowly escaped the powerful gust of Godzilla's strong lungs, which sent cars and vending machines flying. Godzilla's massive jaw snapped inches from the cab. Phillipe raced into a tunnel.

The exit was sealed!

"Now what do we do?" Animal asked.

The cab radio crackled to life. It was Sergeant O'Neal. "Nick, listen," he instructed. "You have to lure him out into the open so we can get a clear shot."

Nick thought. There was a suspension bridge in Brooklyn. That would be perfect. But Godzilla's head blocked the exit.

"This thing have high beams?" Nick asked.

Phillipe understood immediately. He gunned the car directly into Godzilla. At the last moment, he flashed the headlights and slammed on the horn.

It worked! Godzilla was startled, blinded by the bright lights. The car sped through Godzilla's legs…and headed for the bridge.

Godzilla caught them on the entrance ramp, biting down on the cab. Godzilla's tongue pushed through the cab's back window. Acting quickly, Nick spotted a downed electrical cable hanging nearby. He wrapped a jacket around his hand, grabbed the cable, and jammed it into Godzilla's mouth. Sparks flew. The painful shock forced Godzilla to drop the cab. The tires spun, burned, and caught. Phillipe raced to safety.

Still moving forward, injured, weakened, Godzilla tried to cross the great bridge. A squadron of F-18s swooped toward the target. Like a fly trapped in a web, Godzilla became hopelessly entangled in the bridge's suspension wires. The beast struggled to free himself.

Now Godzilla was an easy target. The pilots fired missile after missile into the helpless reptile. Godzilla let out a final, anguished wail, attempted a last step, and crashed to the ground. The beast was dead.

Nick looked at the fallen creature and felt pity. He was an animal, not a monster — an animal that lived the only way he knew, according to the laws of nature. He sought food, shelter, a nesting place. His only crime: Godzilla made the mistake of running into humankind.

All around the destroyed animal, people cheered and slapped one another's backs. A thick pack of reporters, hungry for a story, swarmed around our heroes. "Sorry, guys," Nick said, winking at Audrey. "I've promised my story as an exclusive to another reporter."

Crack...

But wait.

In the vast darkness of Madison Square Garden...beneath the rubble...deeper and deeper into the darkest crevice...lies an egg.

One egg: solitary, unharmed, safe.

Crack. It opens....

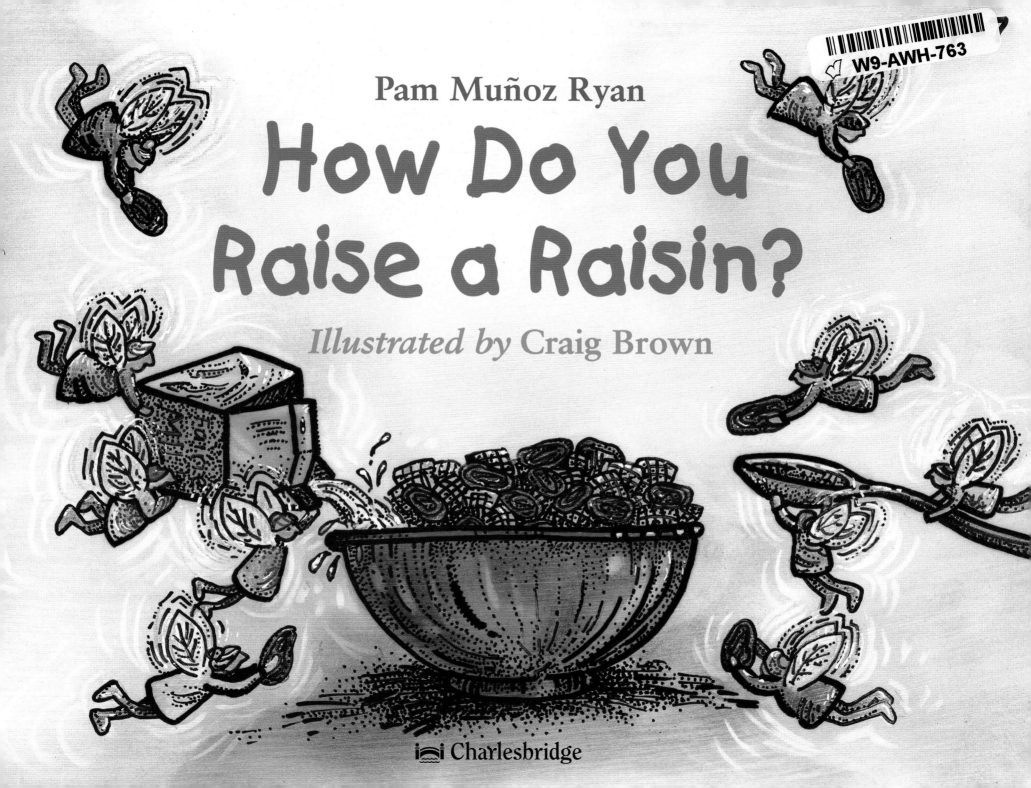

Pam Muñoz Ryan

How Do You Raise a Raisin?

Illustrated by Craig Brown

ini Charlesbridge

To Virginia E. Ford, who was hungry for this book—Pam

For Mary, Beth, and Jane SPRINKLE, SPRINKLE—C.B.

How do you raise a raisin?

Tell me so I'll know.

They're such peculiar little things.

How do they sprout and grow?

Do raisins grow on Earth, or other planets, far away?

Do aliens collect them and space-shuttle them our way?

Raisins are dried grapes. So far, there is no proof
that raisins grow on other planets. Raisins ARE
grown on Earth, in countries like Turkey, Iran,
Greece, Australia, and the United States.

So, who discovered raisins?
Were they here when Earth began?
Who **WAS** the first to nibble them—dinosaur or man?

Raisins were probably discovered when someone
or someTHING tasted grapes that had dried on
the vine. Over the years people and animals
figured out which grapes produced the sweetest,
yummiest raisins.

Do raisins grow in **one** place,
like Raisin Creek or Raisin Hill?
Is there a special town called
Raisinfield or Raisinville?

Raisins grow best in areas with nice dirt, many days of hot weather, a dry climate, and plenty of water. Almost all of the raisins in the United States are grown in the San Joaquin Valley of California, near towns like Chowchilla, Dinuba, Kingsburg, Selma, Weedpatch, and even Raisin City! About 90 percent of the raisins sold in the United States come from the area around Fresno, California.

Raisinville, USA

Do farmers plant some seeds
from the local garden shop?
And wait for raisin bushes
to produce a raisin crop?

Farmers start a new crop of raisins by taking "cuttings"
from an older grapevine. These pieces of stem are planted
in sand until they sprout. Then, they are planted in the fields,
next to a wooden stake.

Notice how the grapevines
and the sprawling branches grow.
Does a grapevine tamer train them
into picture-perfect rows?

Grapevines are grown about eight feet apart. Fieldworkers hand-tie the sturdy branches, or "canes," to rows of wire. There are usually two sets of wire, a top set that is about six feet high, and a second wire that is three or four feet high.

How long do raisins take to grow?
A week, a month, or a year?
How many hours must you wait
for a raisin to appear?

It takes at least three years until the vines are old enough for the first crop of raisins. That's 26,280 hours!

When grapes are ripe and ready,
how do farmers get them down?
Do they rent a burly giant
to shake them to the ground?

When the grapes are ready, skilled grape-pickers snag the grape clusters from the vines using a sharp vine-cutter.

Most grapes are turned into raisins the same way they've been for thousands of years: they are left to dry naturally in the sun.

What do raisins lie on
while they're basking in the sun?
Do they rest on little beach towels
until they're dried and done?

The grape clusters are laid on brown paper trays on the ground between the grapevine rows. This is called "laying the grapes down." The sun rises in the east and sets in the west. Most raisin growers plant their vineyards in east-to-west rows. This way, grapes drying between the rows receive the most sun. If they were drying in north-to-south rows, the grapes would be in the shade part of the day, and when it comes to raising raisins, the more sun the better.

How long do clusters lie around to sweeten, dry, and bake?
How many weeks in the valley heat does raisin-making take?

Raisins bake in the sun for about two to three weeks. Then, the paper trays are rolled into bundles that look like burritos and are left in the field for a few more days to make sure that all the raisins are as dry.

Raisins do not look like grapes—
they're withered up and wrinkled!
Are they soaked inside a bathtub
until their skin is crinkled?

As grapes bake in the hot sun, their water evaporates. The more water they lose, the more the grapes shrivel, causing wrinkles.

How many grapes must a farmer dry
upon the valley ground?
To make a box of raisins
that weighs about one pound?

It takes about four and one-half pounds of fresh
grapes to make one pound of raisins.

How do the raisins get from fields
to the raisin factory door?
Does a vacuum cleaner suck them up
from the dusty valley floor?

Farmworkers toss the raisin bundles into
a wooden trailer. The raisins are sent
across a shaker that gets rid of the dirt
and rocks. Then, raisins are taken to the
factory and stored in big boxes, called
bins, until they are ready to be packaged.

Who puts raisins in the boxes
that keep them sweet and dried?
Do tiny fairy princesses
stuff each one inside?

ENCHANTED
FARMS RAISINS

When they're needed,
raisin bins are brought into
the factory for packaging. It takes
only 10 minutes from bin to package!
Workers and machines take off the stems and
capstems, sort, and wash the raisins. Then the
raisins are packaged in a variety of boxes and bags.

What happens to the raisins
that aren't the very best?
Are they sent to raisin prep school
until they pass the test?

1. Get plenty of sun.
2. Roll over after two weeks.
3. Dry evenly.

When it comes to raisins, nothing is wasted! The stems and capstems are ground up and used for animal feed. Raisins that are not perfect are made into raisin concentrate that's used as a natural preservative in cakes, breads, and cookies. The best raisins are used for eating, baking, and adding to cereals.

Raisins taste so very sweet,
but they're considered "sugar-free."
Is each one dipped in a honey pot
by a busy honeybee?

Raisins are naturally sweet!

What's so great about raisins, anyway?

- They're nutritious. Raisins are rich in iron, calcium, potassium, and B vitamins and provide a good source of fiber.

- They make other foods taste better. Raisins have tartaric acid, a flavor-enhancer. Raisin juice and raisin paste are used in a variety of sauces such as pasta, barbecue, and steak sauces to boost their flavor.

- Raisin paste is sometimes used as filler in meatballs and meat pies to provide more servings.

- Raisins have a rich, natural color. Raisin juice is often added to frozen dairy desserts and baked goods as a color-enhancer, or food coloring.

- Ground raisins can be used instead of fat in fat-free baked goods like fat-free muffins, cookies, and brownies.

- Raisin paste and raisin juice concentrate are mold-inhibitors that prevent food from spoiling as easily. Bakers often use raisin products instead of artificial preservatives. Have you noticed that raisin bread lasts longer than other breads? Raisins extend the shelf life of bakery goods by several days over products without raisin products.

So, now you know how raisins grow.
Here's a little raisin history:

Between 1200–900 B.C., the ancient Phoenicians produced muscat raisins in Spain, so called because they were made from muscat grapes with their distinctive musk odor. The Phoenicians also made tiny raisins from small seedless grapes grown near Corinth, Greece. Called *raisin de Corauntz* by the French, they eventually became known as currants.

Hmmm, tangy and tasty.

Let's put them in the bread.

About the same time, Armenians grew a special seedless grape in Persia (Iraq, Iran, and Turkey). Historians say they were grown specifically for the rulers of the day, the sultans, so these raisins were called sultanas.

First Place! A parcel of raisins! What, no gold medal?

The early Greeks and Romans valued raisins so much that they were given as prizes in sporting events.

The Romans started using raisins in trade and the dried fruit became so valuable that they could be used to purchase just about anything.

Let's see, two pots of raisins, I can get a new toga, new sandals, and an arm bracelet for Mom.

Take nine raisins and call me in the morning.

I'm feeling a little old today, Doctor.

Doctors of ancient Rome and Greece began using raisins to treat all sorts of problems, from joint aches to old age.

The ancient general, Hannibal, who fought a war against Rome in the 200s B.C., fed raisins to his troops as they crossed the Alps.

Raisins didn't become popular in Europe until the 11th century when knights returning home from the Crusades brought raisins back with them from the Mediterranean and Persia.

Daddy, Daddy! Did you bring me a catapult?

No, son, but I brought you raisins.

Grape growing and raising raisins spread to France, Germany, and Spain. Then, in the 18th century, Spanish missionaries brought grape stock (pieces of grapevines) and the knowledge of grape growing (viticulture) to Mexico and what is now California.

Over the years, raising raisins flourished, but raisin seeds were a problem. When seeds were removed the raisins became a sticky, clumpy mess. Bakers and people who liked to eat raisins found this troublesome. They hoped for a seedless grape that would produce a yummy raisin.

In 1876, William Thompson introduced the Lady de Coverly grape to California. The green grapes were seedless, with thin skins, and produced a sweet and flavorful raisin. These grapes changed the raisin-producing industry forever and are still known today as Thompson Seedless grapes. Today 95 percent of the California raisin crop is Thompson Seedless grapes.

For centuries, from Hannibal to the astronauts, people have valued raisins. Scientists who planned the space shuttle menus knew that raisins are the perfect fast food for long journeys. They are lightweight, don't spoil easily, satisfy the craving for something sweet, and provide nutrition and energy.

Ants on a Log

Spread celery pieces with
   peanut butter, cream cheese,
   or cheese spread.
Top with raisins.

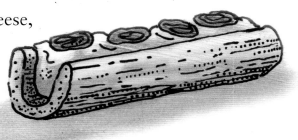

Rats on a Raft

Spread cream cheese on graham crackers.
Dot raisins on top.

Super Balls

1 cup honey
1 ½ cups powdered milk
1 cup peanut butter
1 ½ cups graham cracker crumbs
1 cup raisins
¾ cup crushed corn flakes or dried coconut

Put crushed corn flakes or coconut in a dish.
In a mixing bowl, mix all other ingredients.
Shape into balls.
Roll balls in crushed cornflakes or coconut.

The author wishes to thank the California Raisin Advisory Board, the Selma Chamber of Commerce, Sun-Maid Growers of California, the Serra Research Center of the Serra Cooperative Library System, the California Farm Bureau, Marla Woodcock, and the California Foundation for Agriculture in the Classroom.

Published by Charlesbridge
85 Main Street
Watertown, MA 02472
(617) 926-0329
www.charlesbridge.com

Library of Congress Cataloging-in-Publication Data
Ryan, Pam Muñoz.
   How do you raise a raisin?/ Pam Muñoz Ryan; illustrated by Craig Brown.
   p. cm.
   ISBN-13: 978-1-57091-397-6 (reinforced for library use)
   ISBN-10: 1-57091-397-8 (reinforced for library use)
   ISBN-13: 978-1-57091-398-3 (softcover)
   ISBN-10: 1-57091-398-6 (softcover)
   1. Raisins—Juvenile literature. [1. Raisins.]
I. Brown, Craig McFarland, ill. II. Title.
SB399.R93   2002
664'.8048—dc21   2001028263

Printed in Korea
(hc) 10 9 8 7 6 5 4 3 2
(sc) 10 9 8 7 6 5 4 3

Illustrations done in marker and pastels
Display type and text type set in Catchup and Adobe Sabon
Color separated, printed, and bound by Sung In Printing, South Korea
Production supervision by Brian G. Walker
Designed by Diane M. Earley and Susan Sherman